Chestnut

Written by
Constance W. McGeorge

Illustrated by
Mary Whyte

PEACHTREE
ATLANTA

For Uncle Lou and Aunt Millie.

—*C. W. M.*

For Charleston—my city by the sea.

—*M. W.*

Published by
PEACHTREE PUBLISHERS
1700 Chattahoochee Avenue
Atlanta, Georgia 30318-2112
www.peachtree-online.com

ISBN 1-56145-321-8

Text © 2004 by Constance W. McGeorge
Illustrations © 2004 by Mary Whyte

Illustrations created in watercolor on 100% rag paper. Titles and text typeset in Goudy Infant.

Printed in China
10 9 8 7 6 5 4 3 2 1
First Edition

Library of Congress Cataloging-in-Publication Data
McGeorge, Constance W.
Chestnut / written by Constance McGeorge ; illustrated by Mary Whyte.-- 1st ed.
p. cm.
Summary: When his owner falls asleep, Chestnut the horse makes sure that
the deliveries for Jenny's birthday party arrive on time.
ISBN 1-56145-321-8
[1. Horses--Fiction. 2. Birthdays--Fiction.] I. Whyte, Mary, ill. II. Title.
PZ7.M478467Che 2004
[E]--dc22
2004001982

A long time ago, in a city by the
sea, there lived a horse named Chestnut.

Chestnut belonged to Mr. Decker, who ran a delivery service. Each morning at dawn, Mr. Decker harnessed Chestnut to his wagon. Next, he loaded it with packages. When the clock on the square struck six loud *bongs,* Mr. Decker climbed onto the wagon.

"Walk on!" he said to Chestnut, and the two of them were on their way. They made deliveries to the same places day in and day out. Each morning, they stopped at the baker's, the hat-maker's, the candy shop, and the mayor's house. Every afternoon, they went to the bookshop, the butcher's, the tailor's, and the inn.

One day, after their morning delivery route was done, Mr. Decker and Chestnut returned to the stable as usual. Waiting to see them were a man and a little girl. They were dressed in fine clothes, standing by a handsome carriage. It was the mayor and his daughter, Jenny.

"Good morning, Mayor," said Mr. Decker. "And good day to you, Jenny. Are you excited about your birthday tomorrow?"

"Oh yes, I am," Jenny replied. "And, I'm glad you're coming to my party!" She petted Chestnut's nose. He lowered his head and nickered softly.

"Good morning, Mr. Decker," said the mayor, smiling. He was one of Mr. Decker's oldest friends and best customers. "Can you still make tomorrow morning's deliveries on time?" the mayor asked quietly, glancing at his daughter.

"Of course!" Mr. Decker assured him. "We don't want to disappoint Jenny."

At dawn the next morning, Mr. Decker leapt out of bed and went to the stable.

"Wake up, Chestnut!" he said. "We must be on time today. It's Jenny's big day! Everyone is depending on us." Mr. Decker quickly fed and groomed Chestnut. Then, he harnessed him to the wagon and loaded it with the morning's deliveries.

There was a bag of flour for the baker who was baking the birthday cake. There was a box of bows for the hatmaker who was making Jenny's birthday bonnet. There was a sack of sugar for the candymaker who was creating sweets for the birthday party guests. There was a punch bowl to be delivered to the mayor's house.

And of course, there were birthday presents for Jenny!

"That's it!" Mr. Decker declared when he finished loading his wagon. He looked at his pocket watch.

"It's not yet six, Chestnut," said Mr. Decker. "A little too early to head out. The shopkeepers are just waking up. We'll wait a bit before we start." He sat in a chair and leaned back, closing his eyes—just for a moment.

Chestnut stood at attention, his head high and his eyes bright. He waited and waited for Mr. Decker to climb on the wagon. Finally, Chestnut swung his head to the side and looked at his owner. Mr. Decker was fast asleep.

Then, the clock in the tower began to strike.

Bong.

Chestnut's ears perked up. Mr. Decker didn't move.

Bong.

Chestnut jangled his harness. Mr. Decker didn't hear a sound.

Bong.

Chestnut stomped his hooves. Mr. Decker kept on sleeping.

Bong.

Chestnut whinnied as loud as he could. Mr. Decker snored on and on.

Bong.

Chestnut took one last look at Mr. Decker.

Bong.

Chestnut walked on—all by himself!

Clip, clop, clip, clop.

Chestnut headed down the crooked narrow street. Soon, salty air tickled his nose. It was time to turn south on the harbor side road. But as Chestnut made his way toward his first stop, fog rolled in from the sea.

Familiar sights suddenly disappeared from view. Chestnut slowed to a walk, then a stop. Mr. Decker had always guided him through the fog. Chestnut moved his head from side to side and twitched his nose. And then, it came to him—a warm and familiar smell.

He walked slowly forward.

When Chestnut reached the baker's, he shook his head, jangling his harness. In a moment, the door opened with a bang. The baker rushed outside, into the fog.

"Good morning, Mr. Decker," he said, shaking flour off his hands. "Glad to see you're on time. I've a birthday cake to bake this morning!" He grabbed the bag of flour off the wagon, and not waiting for a reply, hurried back to the bakery.

Chestnut walked on.

Through the misty fog, Chestnut turned the corner and continued, his iron shoes clattering over the cobblestone street. Suddenly, his hooves sank into deep mud. The cobbles had been removed for repairs. The wagon was stuck!

Chestnut lowered his head, leaned hard into his harness, and pressed forward again and again. The wagon wouldn't budge. Then, he took a step back, and another, until the wagon rocked backward. Chestnut tried one more time, as hard as he could, to pull the wagon out of the mud. This time, the wagon lurched forward.

He was on his way again!

Next, Chestnut stopped in front of the hatmaker's shop. He lowered his head to drink from the water trough. The hatmaker dashed outside and went straight to the rear of the wagon.

"Thank you, Mr. Decker," she sang out as she snatched up the box of bows. "Now I can finish Jenny's birthday bonnet! See you at the party," she called over her shoulder. She turned and scurried back to her shop, too rushed to notice Chestnut was alone.

When Chestnut heard the door shut, he walked on.

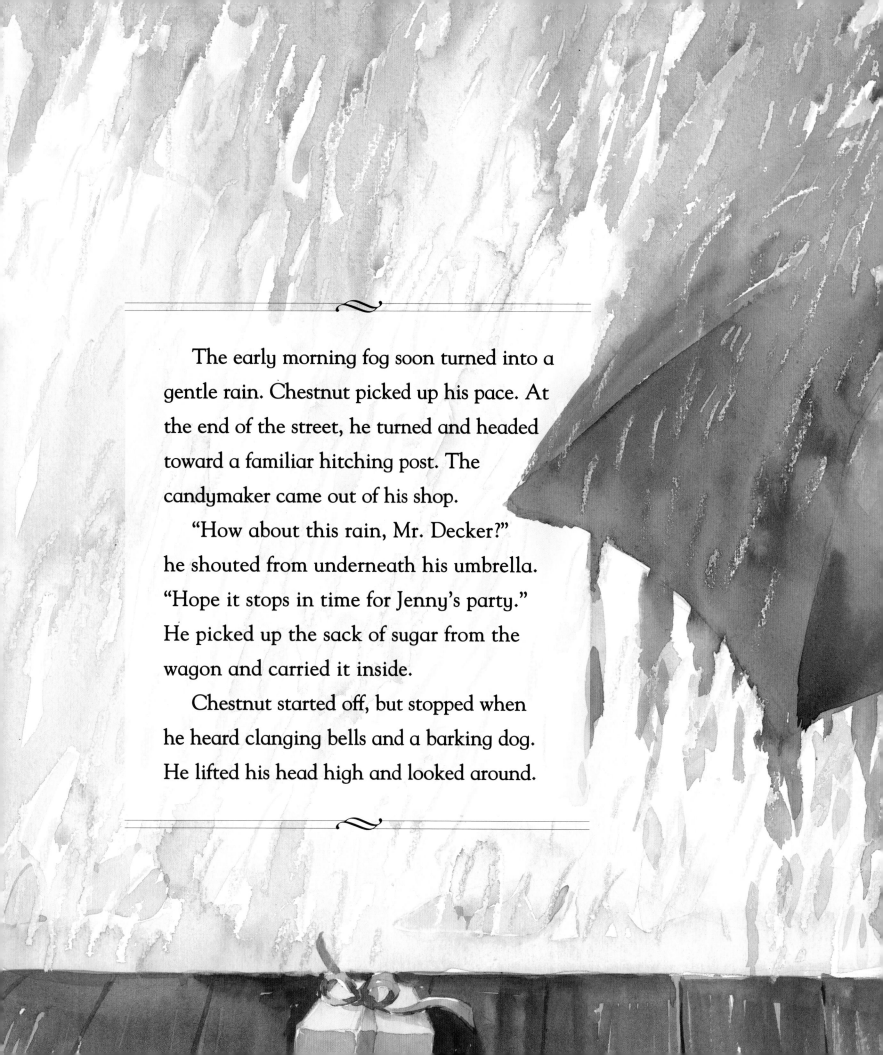

The early morning fog soon turned into a gentle rain. Chestnut picked up his pace. At the end of the street, he turned and headed toward a familiar hitching post. The candymaker came out of his shop.

"How about this rain, Mr. Decker?" he shouted from underneath his umbrella. "Hope it stops in time for Jenny's party." He picked up the sack of sugar from the wagon and carried it inside.

Chestnut started off, but stopped when he heard clanging bells and a barking dog. He lifted his head high and looked around.

Two huge horses came galloping around the corner. While other horses might have shied at the thundering pair, Chestnut knew just what to do. He pulled the wagon aside and waited. The team of fire horses raced past.

When the street was clear, Chestnut trotted quietly along. *Clip, clop, clip, clop.* He came to a row of grand houses and slowed to a walk. Chestnut swung his ears back and forth. He heard a dog barking and came to a halt. It was the mayor's house and the last stop of the morning.

The mayor's housekeeper rubbed her sleepy eyes as she unloaded the punch bowl and the presents.

"Thank goodness the bowl didn't break," she said between yawns. "We'll see you at the party, Mr. Decker."

As he walked on, Chestnut felt the lightness of the wagon. It was time to head home.

By the time Chestnut turned down the crooked narrow street to Mr. Decker's stable, the rain and fog had lifted in the city by the sea, and the morning sun peeked through pale gray clouds. Chestnut broke into a brisk trot.

The clatter of Chestnut's shoes on the stable floor and the rattle of the empty wagon woke Mr. Decker. He looked at his pocket watch and jumped up in dismay.

"Oh no," Mr. Decker exclaimed. "The deliveries are late!" He started toward the wagon, then looked at Chestnut, still warm from work and wet with rain.

"Wait! You were dry a moment ago," Mr. Decker said. He looked inside the wagon and frowned. "Oh dear, oh dear, where are the packages?" Chestnut nuzzled Mr. Decker and nickered softly.

Just then, there was a knock at the stable door. It was the mayor and Jenny. "Hello, Mr. Decker," said Jenny. "I came to say thank you to Chestnut!"

Mr. Decker looked out the door at Jenny and the mayor, and at the wet cobblestone street beyond them. He saw the smile on Jenny's face. Suddenly, Mr. Decker understood. Chestnut had made all the deliveries that morning! Mr. Decker patted his faithful horse and beamed with pride.

And so that sunny afternoon, there was a party in the city by the sea. Everyone there celebrated Jenny's birthday—and a horse named Chestnut.